The Rescue Princesses

The Moonlight Mystery

More amazing
animal adventures!

The Secret Promise

The Wishing Pearl

The Stolen Crystals

The Rescue Princesses

The Moonlight Mystery

💜 PAULA HARRISON 💜

Scholastic Inc.

For Teri, who was there on the journey

ISBN 978-0-545-50915-2

Previously published as *The Moonlit Mystery*.

12 11   16 17 18/0

Printed in the U.S.A.   40

First printing, August 2013

CHAPTER ONE

Tree Acrobatics

Princess Lulu grasped the lowest branch of the tree with both hands and swung herself backward and forward. After a few swings, she stretched high enough to curl her legs around the branch above.

Her curly black hair swayed as she climbed. She wore a short yellow dress dotted with tiny golden beads. It was her tree-climbing dress, and it was now extremely dusty. On her left hand she wore a ring with a gleaming yellow topaz, her favorite jewel.

Halfway up the tree there was a long straight branch, almost as straight and smooth as the beam in Lulu's gym. She loved practicing in the gym, but being out here with the sun blazing down and the breeze on her face was even better.

On her left stood the palace of Undala, with its courtyard and fountain, and on her right was the outer wall, with the golden grasslands beyond. In the distance, an elephant lifted its trunk at the water hole, getting its early-morning drink.

Lulu smiled and turned back to the branch in front of her. She wanted to see if she could do a cartwheel on it. She stood tall and gazed straight ahead, excitement fizzing inside her. Then, pointing one foot, she raised her arms high above her head, ready to cartwheel.

"Achoo!" The ear-splitting sneeze came from below, making Lulu jump. She wobbled and nearly fell off the branch. Grabbing on to the tree trunk, she peered down toward the ground.

Prince Olaf stood under the tree, his spiky blond head looking up at her. Lulu sighed. Olaf was visiting the kingdom of Undala with his parents, the king and queen of Finia, and ever since arriving he'd been following Lulu around. He'd seemed so nice when she'd met him before, at royal balls and banquets. But now she thought he was a know-it-all!

Olaf sneezed again. "Sorry!" he said. "I was just watching. I love learning acrobatics and circus skills. I was practicing them in your gym yesterday. Maybe I can teach you some?"

Lulu swung down from the branch and landed on the ground in front of him,

hands on her hips. "You were practicing in *my* gym?"

"That's right." Olaf grinned, not noticing Lulu's frown. "I think I'm getting really good at walking the beam."

"Really?" Lulu folded her arms. "How many times did you fall off first?"

"A few times." Olaf didn't look even the tiniest bit embarrassed. "Would you like me to show you how to do it? I can always hold your hand if you're nervous."

Lulu's eyes flashed. Olaf was the most annoying prince she'd ever met! "No thanks!" she snapped. "I can turn hundreds of cartwheels on my beam, and I certainly don't need anyone to hold my hand!" She was about to add that she would show him just how good she was, but the low *clang* of the breakfast gong interrupted her.

Lulu rushed inside, with Olaf trailing behind her. She was going out to the grasslands with Walter, the royal ranger, this morning and she didn't want to be late. She bounded into the palace hallway, with its shelves of beautiful animal carvings. A huge painting of a lion standing at the foot of a mountain hung next to the doorway. Inside the Great Hall, the maids were setting out the breakfast plates. Lulu hurried in and found a seat at the long wooden table.

"Good morning, Lulu. Good morning, Olaf," said Lulu's mom, Queen Shani, with a warm smile. "Have either of you seen Lady Malika?"

Lulu shook her head and helped herself to the warm buttered rolls.

"No, I haven't, Your Majesty," replied Prince Olaf with a sweeping bow. "But I'll go and look for her if you want."

Lady Malika was the queen's sister, who lived on the other side of Undala. It was a long way away, so she didn't visit very often. She owned a big circus in the city, which Lulu had visited once when she was little. Like the Finians, Lady Malika had come to stay at the palace for a few weeks.

"Thank you, Prince Olaf. But there's no need. I just wondered where she was because her room is empty," said Queen Shani. "Perhaps she had something important to do this morning, so she left the palace early."

Lulu scowled at Prince Olaf, who was offering the rolls to the queen politely, and wished more than anything that her friends, princesses Emily, Clarabel, and Jaminta, had come to visit instead. She knew they'd love Undala, with its huge grasslands filled with wild animals. She sighed wistfully, just as a horn honked loudly outside the window.

"That's Walter! He must be ready to leave," she cried, racing out of the hall and down the front steps.

"Slow down, Lulu! Do you have to rush everywhere?" the queen called after her.

Lulu jumped into the truck, next to Walter, who smiled at her. "Let's go!" she cried.

They zoomed through the tall palace gates, with the red earth flying beneath their wheels.

CHAPTER TWO

Princess of the Wild

Walter drove them across the rough grasslands, circling carefully around a herd of grazing elephants. "I suppose you want to see the lioness's hollow again?" he said, pushing up the sleeves of his checkered shirt.

"Yes, please!" Lulu's dark eyes sparkled with delight. "Maybe today the cubs will come out to play."

Walter slowed the truck down in front

of a patch of bushes before coming to a stop underneath a tall tree.

"I'm going to check the animals at the water hole," he told her. "Remember what I said about staying in the truck. It's not safe for you to walk around on your own."

Lulu nodded. But as soon as he'd disappeared down the slope, she leapt up from her seat and out of the open-air truck as if waiting one more second would make her burst. She grabbed on to the lowest branch of the tree above her. Hauling herself up, she reached for the next branch and the next, climbing swiftly. At last she stood at the very top, able to see the beautiful kingdom of Undala spread out below her.

Miles of tall golden grass rippled in the wind, and in the distance the black-and-white blur of a zebra herd moved slowly across the plain. But Lulu wasn't interested in zebras. She'd seen them hundreds of times. Her eyes were fixed on a hollow in the sun-baked red earth. A bush right next to the hollow quivered, and a small paw stuck out.

Lulu grinned in delight and crouched down on her branch, hanging on to the tree trunk with one hand. She'd been waiting for this moment for six long weeks, ever since the lioness had made the hollow into her den. Lulu knew all about the animals that roamed near her palace, and she knew that the cubs would be almost ready to come out for the very first time. She was so excited at the thought of actually seeing them!

A low growl came from the hollow, and the lioness sprang into view. She padded out of the bush, sniffing the air in all directions. Satisfied that there was no danger near, she settled down on the

dusty earth and gave another growl. Five little lion cubs skipped out of the hollow, bounding all around their mother. Their golden fur gleamed in the sun. The smallest cub struggled to climb up onto his mother's back. He slipped off over and over again, but finally managed to scramble up and then fell right to sleep at the top.

Lulu smiled as she watched them. Five cubs was a really good-sized litter, and they were so cute. She settled more comfortably on her branch, until footsteps below reminded her that she hadn't come here alone. Walter was shading his eyes as he looked up into the tree.

Lulu waved to him, clambered quickly back down, and dropped into the seat of the truck.

Walter got into the driver's seat and drove off jerkily. "I thought you were going to wait in the truck. It can be dangerous out here," he said.

"I know, I'm sorry, Walter," said Lulu. "But don't worry. I didn't walk around, I just climbed right up the tree. And guess what?" She grinned at the ranger happily. "The lion cubs came out to play and there are five of them!"

Walter grunted. "But you could have fallen out of the tree. What would the king and queen say?"

"I'd never fall out!" said Lulu, laughing. "It's a really easy tree to climb, and it was worth it to see the little cubs. Thanks for letting me come with you."

Walter grunted again and looked at her from under his bushy eyebrows. "You didn't just come along to avoid that prince, then?"

Lulu looked at him solemnly. "It was all about seeing the lion cubs, I promise you."

Walter snorted with laughter and swung the truck around. As the royal ranger, he looked after a vast area of grasslands and the animals that lived there. Lulu knew that he liked her company on the long drives. But he was also right that she was glad to get away from Prince Olaf.

Later on, she would write and tell the other princesses all about the cubs. Together, the four girls had made a secret promise always to help any creature in trouble and had already performed two daring animal rescues. Lulu missed her friends a lot and she knew they'd love to hear about the baby lions. She wished they could see the cubs for themselves.

"We're driving around to the other side of the water hole next," said Walter. "I need to check the number of hippos living there. After that we'll take a look at how far the bison herd has moved."

They spent a long day driving around checking the numbers of animals in the area and making sure that they all looked healthy. As the sun dipped in the sky, they headed back toward the palace for dinner.

"Could we please take one more look at the lion cubs?" begged Lulu. "Just for a minute."

"All right," said Walter. "It's on our way."

They stopped underneath the tree near the lioness's den. The orange sun was setting now, and the bushes next to the hollow were completely still.

Walter took out his binoculars and peered through them. "That's strange," he said. "There's no sign of them at all."

Lulu took the binoculars and took a look. "I'll climb the tree again. I can see the whole den from the top." She swung quickly up the tree, but even from there she saw no sign of the lioness or the cubs.

Frowning, Walter climbed out of the truck and walked toward the bushes. He peered over them for a few moments. Then, shaking his head, he returned to Lulu. "It looks like they're gone," he said.

"Gone?" repeated Lulu. "You mean they've moved to another den?"

"Maybe. But . . ." His frown deepened. "There have been far fewer animals around here lately. There aren't as many zebras or leopards as there should be. I haven't seen them leave. It's almost as if they just disappeared."

"Why would they disappear?" she asked, but Walter shook his head again.

Lulu felt a cold dread grow inside her.

Surely nothing bad had happened to the cubs? Surely the lioness would have protected her babies from danger?

Just then there was a faint cry, almost like a cat meowing, and a scrabbling noise came from behind a rock. Lulu's heart thumped. What could be hiding there? Was it an animal in trouble?

CHAPTER THREE

A Cub Named Tufty

Forgetting all about the danger, Lulu jumped out of the truck and raced over to the rock. Hiding behind it was one little lion cub. He looked at her and gave a mournful yowl. Lulu thought he had the most beautiful brown eyes she'd ever seen.

"You poor little thing!" she said to the cub. "Are you all alone?"

The cub meowed and lifted up one paw.

Lulu turned to Walter with a determined look in her eye. "We have to take him back with us," she said firmly. "He's too young to take care of himself." She picked up the tiny cub and stroked him soothingly.

Walter raised one bushy eyebrow. "If you take him, he'll be your responsibility until we find his family. Do you really want to feed him and look after him?"

"Of course!" cried Lulu.

"Where will you put him?"

"He can sleep with me in my bedroom — that way I can look after him carefully."

Walter sighed and gave in.

They wrapped the lion cub up in a blanket, and he rode back to the palace on Lulu's lap. He squirmed a lot. His ears stayed pricked up and his inquisitive little eyes watched the grasslands rush past him out the window.

"I'm going to call you Tufty," said Lulu, scratching the tufts of fur that stuck up from his ears. Tufty purred deeply and nudged Lulu's hand, closing his eyes blissfully.

The truck slowed down as they approached the gates and the high tangerine walls of the palace came into view. Behind the palace loomed the huge black shape of Shimmer Rock, the only mountain in the kingdom.

When she got inside, Lulu sneaked Tufty, still hidden under the blanket, up to her bedroom. She knew her parents wouldn't like her taking care of a lion cub, but she was sure he was too young to be dangerous. She wasn't going to tell Prince Olaf, either. He was sure to tell on her to the grown-ups. How she wished the other Rescue Princesses were here to help!

She set the little cub down on her bed. He scampered across her duvet, trying to catch a fly with his tiny paws. The fly got away and Tufty rolled over onto his back, waving his legs in the air like he was pretending to swim.

Lulu chuckled. "You're so funny! I know Emily, Clarabel, and Jaminta would love you so much."

Tufty rolled back onto his stomach and looked at her with his big brown eyes.

She stroked his furry ears. "I bet you miss your brothers and sisters, but don't worry. I'll take care of you. Everything will be all right. Walter and I will find your family as soon as we can."

But that evening brought some bad news. Lulu was tiptoeing through the hallway to the kitchen to fetch milk for Tufty, when one of the kitchen maids walked past and saw her.

"Oh, good evening, Your Majesty!" The maid curtsied. "Walter asked me to give you this." She handed Lulu an envelope.

Lulu tore it open and read:

Dear Princess Lulu,

I've been called away for a few days to work on the other side of Undala, near the Great Desert. Take good care of the lion cub. He'll need milk every few hours. Remember not to fall out of any trees!

With all my best wishes,
Walter

Her heart sinking, Lulu climbed back upstairs. She sat down in front of the mirror and stared at the streaks of reddish dust on her face. Who was going to help her find the missing lions now?

She heard softly padding paws behind her. Tufty let out a low meow, leapt into her lap, and curled up, purring.

"Oh, Tufty!" she said. "I forgot your milk!"

But Tufty just closed his eyes and purred. With a sudden ripple of excitement, Lulu knew what she had to do. She didn't have to fix this problem by herself. It was time to call the other Rescue Princesses! They would find the lions together.

She looked in delight at the yellow topaz ring on her finger. Each of the four princesses had their own ring made from a different kind of jewel. But they weren't just ordinary rings. The princesses could use them to call one another for help with an animal rescue. Jaminta had shaped the jewels perfectly to bring out the magic inside them.

Lulu smiled. Now she could find the missing lions *and* see her friends again. She lifted the ring to her lips, pressed the yellow topaz and spoke clearly into the jewel.

"Calling all Rescue Princesses! This is Lulu in the kingdom of Undala. There are animals in trouble here. I repeat: There are animals in trouble."

The yellow topaz glowed brightly for a second. Then a voice came from far away. "This is Jaminta in the kingdom of Onica. I'm on my way to help you."

"Hello, Lulu," came a second voice. "This is Clarabel in Winteria. I'll leave as soon as I can."

There was silence. Lulu waited hopefully.

"This is Emily in the kingdom of Middingland." The third voice sounded very faint. "I wouldn't miss this rescue for anything!"

The yellow topaz glowed once more and the voices were gone. Lulu beamed. She felt like doing hundreds of cartwheels all around the room. But Tufty was sleeping peacefully on her lap, so she contented herself with giving his soft ears another pet.

"The Rescue Princesses will be here soon," she whispered to him. "They'll come as fast as they can." Her heart thumped with excitement.

Then she was struck by a sudden thought. How was she going to explain to her mom and dad that she'd invited her friends to the palace, and that they were already on their way?

CHAPTER FOUR

A Noise in the Night

Lulu frowned, trying to work out what she was going to say to the king and queen. How could she tell them that she needed her friends to visit without giving away their secret? She had to think fast.

Lifting up the sleeping lion cub, Lulu laid him down carefully on her pillow and sneaked out of her room. There were lights on downstairs, so her parents were probably still awake. She hurried down, determined to persuade them to let her friends stay.

The Great Hall was empty, but there were voices outside in the courtyard.

"It's difficult running a circus." Lady Malika's voice was sharp. "It's hard to find new acts that people want to watch."

"Yes, but I think using animals would be the wrong thing to do," said Queen Shani quietly. "A circus really isn't a suitable place for a wild animal to live."

Lulu took a deep breath and marched into the courtyard. Her parents and Lady Malika were sitting next to the fountain, enjoying a cup of Undalan tea.

"Goodness, Lulu!" laughed Lady Malika. "You're up late!"

Queen Shani rose from her seat, her silver crown glittering. "What's the matter? Are you feeling ill?"

Lulu shook her head. "I wanted to ask you something important."

"You're very dusty!" Lady Malika's eyes narrowed. "Have you been out into the grasslands today?"

"Yes, I went in the truck with Walter to check on the animals," Lulu replied.

"What was it you wanted to ask, Lulu?" said the king, his golden turban gleaming in the lamplight.

"I'd like you to invite my friends, princesses Emily, Clarabel, and Jaminta to visit us soon." She hesitated. "Actually, I, er, sort of already told them they could come." She crossed her fingers and hoped her parents wouldn't ask exactly how she'd invited them. She really couldn't give away how the secret rings worked.

"Lulu!" exclaimed Queen Shani. "You really must think a little harder before you rush off and do things like that. Now

I shall have to telephone their parents to explain."

Lady Malika stared at Lulu, her head tilted to one side. "Sister!" she said. "Maybe it would be a good idea to invite these girls to stay. Then they can do princess things together, rather than roaming around the grasslands."

Lulu stared back at Lady Malika. She was grateful that her aunt agreed with her. She just wasn't sure why her aunt had spoken up like that. It was hard to tell what Lady Malika was thinking behind her sharp eyes and half-smiling mouth.

The queen's brown eyes were thoughtful. "Well, it *would* be nice for you to have some friends here," she said at last. "As long as their parents are happy to let them come."

"I'm sure they'll come if you send a

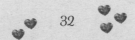

proper royal invitation, sister," said Lady Malika.

The king and queen exchanged glances. "All right, then," said Queen Shani. "The other princesses can come and visit."

"Thank you!" cried Lulu.

The queen raised her hand to quiet her daughter. "But only if you promise us something in return."

"Anything!" said Lulu, her dark eyes lighting up. "I'll do anything."

"The princesses can come as long as you are nicer to Prince Olaf," said the queen.

Lulu groaned. Being nice to Olaf would be really hard work.

"And we want you to take some lessons with Madame Rez," added the king.

"What? Why? Who is she?" asked Lulu.

The queen sighed. "Do try to speak gently, my dear."

"But who is she?" said Lulu.

"Madame Rez is your new etiquette teacher," said the king. "She's here to help you learn proper princess manners."

Lulu made a face. That all sounded very dull, but what choice did she have? "All right, I'll be nice to Prince Olaf and do the new lessons." She dropped into a wobbly curtsy.

Bouncing back upstairs, she forgot all about the promises she'd just made to her parents. The important thing was that the other princesses were coming, and together they would find Tufty's family.

She was about to climb into bed when she heard a noise outside. Padding over to the open window, she looked out into the darkness. The moon was hidden, but the stars made a pattern across the sky like scattered jewels. She began to turn away when a glint caught her eye.

Something winked at the far side of the garden, next to the old gray wall near the gardener's shed.

Holding the fluttering curtain still, she stared hard at the spot. But nothing else happened. Maybe it had been a firefly, or the eyes of a lizard.

Lulu gazed at the little lion cub curled up on her bed. His soft tummy rose and fell as he breathed quietly in his sleep. "Don't worry, little Tufty," she whispered. "The Rescue Princesses are coming. We won't let you down."

Lying her head on the pillow, she closed her eyes and thought of Emily, Clarabel, and Jaminta. The sooner they got here, the sooner all the lions would be back together and happy once again.

CHAPTER FIVE

The Royal Banquet

Lulu hovered by the palace gates, her heart thumping. She scanned the dusty road for any sign of a carriage. All she'd seen so far were gazelles leaping across the grasslands. The queen had made the visit invitation official on the telephone, and Emily, Clarabel, and Jaminta had all flown to the Undalan airport that morning from their different countries.

Lulu wished her dad had sent a car to

pick them up, but he wanted them to have a proper royal welcome.

"All visitors must be greeted by the royal carriage, Lulu," he said. "We can't just send some silly car. It would be wrong."

"It would be faster," said Lulu.

The king smiled and shook his head.

At last, a speck appeared in the distance and grew larger.

Lulu leapt up and down, her eyes sparkling. "They're almost here!"

A golden carriage, driven by two horsemen in purple uniforms, drew up to the palace gates. Three heads leaned out of the carriage window, one red haired, one black haired, and one golden haired.

"Hey, Lulu!" called the princesses. "We're here!" They waved to her excitedly.

"I'm so happy to see you!" shouted Lulu, waving back.

At last, the carriage stopped at the palace steps and the three princesses climbed out eagerly. They were followed by Ally, Emily's maid, who had come to look after them.

"Welcome to the kingdom of Undala," said Queen Shani, smiling at them all.

Emily's red curls bounced as she curtsied. "Thank you, Your Majesty. I bring good wishes from the kingdom of Middingland."

"We're so pleased to come and visit," Clarabel said shyly, her blue eyes and blond hair shining. "I also have good wishes, from the land of Winteria."

"My greetings come from the kingdom of Onica. Thank you for inviting us," added Jaminta, her straight dark hair falling to her shoulders.

Lulu jumped up the palace steps,

bursting with energy. "Great! Now that that's all finished, come this way, girls."

"Just a minute," said the king, laughing. "The princesses must be introduced to our other visitors, then there will be a royal banquet to celebrate their arrival."

Lulu sighed. Banquets always took so long. She just wanted to talk to the princesses in secret and start making a rescue plan.

"We'll have time to catch up later," said Emily, winking at her.

"Right — later!" Lulu grinned and winked back.

So after they'd been introduced to everyone, the princesses went upstairs to put on their best ball gowns and favorite tiaras. Lulu was impatient for them to meet Tufty, but she knew she would have to wait until after dinner. They met in the hallway next to the huge lion picture and waited for the dinner gong to sound.

Emily wore a pink satin ball gown, while Clarabel's was pale blue and shimmered in the light. Jaminta wore a dress of wonderfully smooth green silk. Their special rings sparkled on their fingers. Emily's ring was a red ruby, Jaminta's was a green emerald, and Clarabel's was a sapphire of the deepest blue.

Lulu's golden tiara matched her golden dress, which swished around her as she moved. Her yellow topaz ring twinkled. She grinned at her friends. "I've got so much to tell you," she said. "I hope dinner doesn't take too long."

"I got here as fast as I could," Emily told her. "I begged my parents to let me pack as soon as your message came through!"

"The rings worked really well," said Lulu, smiling at Jaminta. "Prince Olaf asked me why I wore mine all the time, but I wouldn't tell him."

"We saw lots of animals through the carriage windows," said Clarabel. "I've never seen giraffes before. They're so tall and so graceful."

"But which animal is in danger, Lulu?" asked Emily. "You didn't tell us in your message."

Lulu's face clouded over. "A lioness and four of her cubs have gone missing. No one knows why. Walter, the palace ranger, thinks other animals have disappeared, too. Something really strange is going on."

"What's really strange?" said Prince Olaf, coming down the stairs.

Lulu scowled and nearly said something rude. Then she remembered her promise to her parents. With a huge effort, she turned to Olaf. "It's strange that the banquet hasn't started yet, that's all."

Just then, the kings and queens and Lady Malika arrived, dressed in their fanciest robes and crowns. The king and queen of Finia had fair hair, just like Olaf, and wore velvet robes that hung down to the floor. Lady Malika wore a long black dress and her hair was decorated with bright feathers.

"Good evening, Your Majesties!" Prince Olaf gave them a huge bow, providing them all a close-up of the top of his spiky blond head. "And good evening, princesses."

The princesses curtsied in response.

The queen of Undala nodded approvingly. "You have lovely manners, Prince Olaf."

Lulu rolled her eyes. Why couldn't her mom see how annoying Olaf was?

The gong sounded for dinner and they all trooped into the Great Hall. The long table was laden with delicious food

served in golden dishes. Lulu, who had
been too excited about seeing her friends
to eat very much all day, suddenly realized
how hungry she was. She grinned as
Emily sat down next to her, and groaned
inwardly as Prince Olaf sat down on her
other side.

"I'd love to go and see some wildlife
tomorrow," said Olaf loudly. "I thought I
saw a squirrel earlier and it'd be great to
see some more."

Lulu rolled her eyes again and took
a huge bite of dinner so that she didn't
have to reply. Did he seriously think
squirrels lived in Undala?

"Actually, we don't have any squirrels in
our country," said Queen Shani. "But it's
a lovely idea for you to see the wildlife.
I'm sure Lulu will take you."

Lulu shot a look of dismay at the other
princesses. The last thing she wanted was

to be stuck with Olaf when there were animals to help!

"You must go look at Shimmer Rock as well," said the king of Undala. "There are stories about the mountain going back hundreds of years."

"What do the stories say?" asked Emily.

"Shimmer Rock is supposed to be a hollow mountain with magic inside — so the old tales go. It shimmers in the moonlight, just like its name says. People used to think the lights were pixies having a party in the night." The king chuckled at the thought of it. "Of course, it's all made up. But the place is still worth a visit. After all, it's the only mountain in Undala."

Lulu sighed. All this talking was just slowing things down. But she perked up as bowls full of sweet Undalan pudding were brought in for dessert. The pudding had juicy chunks of mango in it. Lulu smiled and scooped it up quickly. Mango pudding was her favorite.

The king of Finia leaned forward. "I hear that you run a circus, Lady Malika. That must be very exciting. Our son, Olaf, is interested in acrobatics."

Lady Malika nodded. "It keeps me busy. There's always so much to do."

"I once heard of a circus that had performing elephants," interrupted Olaf.

The princesses stared at him in shock. How could people make wild animals do tricks in a circus? It was horrible.

"We don't have animals in the circus in Undala," said Queen Shani. "It isn't allowed. But we like acrobatics and clowns very much."

Lady Malika frowned a little and helped herself to more dessert.

Lulu stifled a yawn. The kings and

queens could talk for ages. "May we go now?" she asked.

Queen Shani nodded, so the four princesses curtsied and hurried up the stairs, their dresses swirling as they climbed. When they reached Lulu's room, a scratching noise from behind the door made Emily, Jaminta, and Clarabel back away, wide-eyed.

"Don't worry!" said Lulu, grinning. "It's just a friend of mine. He's staying here for a while."

"Really?" said Clarabel nervously.

Lulu gently swung the door open, and there was the lion cub, his eyes shining and his whiskers quivering. He sprang over to Lulu, twisting in and out of her legs and purring.

Lulu saw her friends' surprised faces and laughed. "Girls! I'd like you to meet Tufty."

CHAPTER SIX

Tracking the Lions

Lulu told the princesses how she'd secretly brought Tufty to the palace after the other lions had disappeared. Then Emily, Clarabel, and Jaminta cooed over him, all wanting to pet him at the same time.

The little cub became very excited about all the attention and started leaping onto the bed and jumping off again, sending the girls into fits of giggles. At last, Clarabel, who seemed to soothe him the best, managed to settle him down with some warm milk in a baby bottle from the kitchen. After that, he snuggled up on her lap, still wide awake but quiet.

"It's a good thing he's such a young cub. Those claws will become sharp in a few weeks' time," said Jaminta.

"I think he's lovely!" Clarabel squeezed him tight. "But you're right, Jaminta. He's still a wild animal, and he'll need to be back with his family soon."

"Where should we look for them?" asked Emily.

Lulu sighed. "I don't know. The hollow where they lived is empty. There's no sign of them at all."

Emily pushed back her red curls. "Maybe we can go back there and look around for clues. I've heard that tracking is an important ninja skill. Why don't I ask Ally if she can show us how to do it?"

Lulu sat up straight, her heart beating faster. "Great idea! Let's take Ally out with us tomorrow morning."

All the princesses trusted Emily's maid, Ally, completely. She'd helped them perform animal rescues before and would never give away their secrets. Besides being excellent at polishing tiaras and cleaning ball gowns, Ally also had unusual skills from her previous job. Before she began working at the palace in Middingland, she had been an undercover agent who caught jewel thieves. The princesses had used the ninja skills she'd taught them several times.

Early the following morning, the princesses tiptoed down the stairs. A faint orange light had just begun to seep into the dawn sky and the palace lay completely silent. The four girls sneaked into the kitchen and gathered rolls and juice for their safari breakfast. As they crept through the hall, Clarabel accidentally bumped into the enormous dinner gong. Only Lulu's speedy dive to grab it stopped the whole palace from being woken by a deafening chime.

Stifling their giggles, the girls ran out to the truck, where Ally was sitting. Then she drove them quickly toward the palace gates.

"Duck!" hissed Lulu as they passed the front entrance.

The princesses crouched down in their seats, making themselves as small as possible. The gates passed by on either side, and they drove out into the wilderness beyond.

"What happened? Why did we have to hide?" asked Jaminta, climbing back up onto the seat.

"It was Prince Olaf." Lulu grimaced. "He was staring at us from an upstairs window."

Emily looked surprised. "Does it really matter if he saw us?"

"My parents wanted me to take him out to see the animals, remember?" said Lulu gloomily. "He'll ruin everything if he comes along."

Clarabel tucked her golden hair behind her ears. "Don't you like Prince Olaf, Lulu? I've always thought he was really nice."

"He seems friendly," added Emily.

"You don't know how awful it's been," Lulu said darkly. "Every time I do something, he's there, trying to do it first. He thinks he knows everything. And the other day" — she paused for effect — "he said he'd been playing on my gymnastics equipment!"

The other princesses burst out laughing.

"You're funny, Lulu!" said Emily. "It sounds like he's just trying to be friends with you."

But Lulu shook her head. "I'm so glad you're here now. Prince Olaf was driving me crazy!"

They stopped for a moment to let a herd of zebras gallop past, then they drove on across the rough ground. The sun rose higher in the sky. Soon they reached Lulu's tree, right next to the lion cubs' hollow.

"This is the right place." Lulu swallowed a lump in her throat as she thought of the little cubs playing together. "There were five cubs and a lioness. Then, when I came back later, only Tufty was left."

Ally told them to look around carefully with binoculars before leaving the truck. Once they were sure that no dangerous animals were prowling nearby, they got out and walked over to the hollow.

"Are these the lions' paw prints?" asked Jaminta, looking closely at some marks in the earth.

Lulu crouched down. "These are the cubs' prints, and these are the lioness's," she said, pointing them out.

She followed the paw prints through the thick bushes and out the other side, right up to where the trail met long swaths of golden grass. She called out to the others, her heart thumping. "Look, everyone! The tracks lead away from the den right into the grasslands!"

CHAPTER SEVEN

Manners and Mischief

"Can you still see the tracks under all that grass?" asked Clarabel.

Lulu waded in. "It's a little bit harder, but I can still see them."

"One moment, Your Majesties," said Ally, crouching down in the hollow. "See these tracks? They're really close together." She walked along the trail. "And here the paw prints get farther and farther apart."

"What does that mean?" said Emily.

Ally stood up, shading her eyes with her hand. "When the tracks get farther apart, it means the animals started to run."

"Maybe they ran because something scared them," suggested Clarabel.

Lulu called to them from the long grass. "Look at this! The tracks go up to here and then they just stop. There's nothing else."

The others rushed over to look.

"You're right, they do just stop," said Jaminta. "I wonder why."

They all stared at the last set of paw prints, half-hidden by the grass. Even Ally shook her head.

"Poor cubs! At least there's no sign they were hurt," said Clarabel.

"But how did they just vanish?" cried Emily. "It doesn't make any sense."

Lulu scanned the horizon, tears pricking her eyes. Giraffes were nibbling leaves

from the treetops. An elephant stood by the water hole. But there were no lion cubs.

"I hope we can find them," said Clarabel.

"We *will* find them!" said Lulu fiercely. "Rescue Princesses never, ever give up."

Climbing back into the truck, Ally and the princesses used a map of the grasslands to plan out where to search. Then, hot, tired, and covered in red dust, they drove back to the palace. Lulu was having her first lesson with her new etiquette teacher after lunch, and Ally insisted she shouldn't be late.

Lulu frowned as she changed out of her comfortable dress and put on the one she was supposed to wear for the lesson. It was a wide-skirted ball gown that hung down to her ankles. She stared at its frilly edges in the mirror. She liked shorter dresses better. This one would be totally useless for somersaulting.

The lesson began downstairs in a room next to the palace courtyard. Madame Rez was a skinny, gray-haired lady who looked Lulu up and down through little round glasses. Then she made Lulu practice standing up and sitting down over and over, telling her each time what she was doing wrong.

"To be really ladylike, you must have good manners. Hold your skirt like this," said Madame Rez, lifting one corner of her long gown. "Then place one leg behind the other as you carefully lower yourself to a seated position."

Lulu sighed, grabbed her dress, and plonked herself down on the chair.

"No, no, no!" Madame Rez clutched her face in horror. "Those are not the manners of a princess! Keep your back

straight and lift the skirt delicately, like this."

Lulu grimaced and pulled her tiara down over her forehead. She knew she should try harder, but it seemed like such a waste of time. She longed to get back outside and continue the search for the lions. She sat down on the chair, swinging her legs and looking out the window.

"Next we will practice how to sit still on a chair," declared Madame Rez.

Lulu groaned.

By the end of an hour, she still hadn't managed to sit down and stay still in a way that made Madame Rez happy. She felt frustrated and hot and just about ready to leap out of the window.

"Let us try standing straight by balancing a book on the head," said Madame Rez. "There is so much I must teach you to make you ladylike!"

Lulu's mouth dropped open. She'd already lasted an hour. Surely it was time to stop! She had to find a way to make Madame Rez let her go.

Just then, there was a faint scratching at the window that looked out over the courtyard.

"What was that?" asked Madame Rez sharply. "We cannot have any interruptions."

The scratching grew louder, and a deep purring made the window pane rattle.

Lulu turned around to catch a glimpse of big brown eyes and silky whiskers pressed up against the glass. Then the creature's mouth opened to reveal two rows of large, pointed teeth.

CHAPTER EIGHT

Tufty Finds a Hiding Place

"A wild beast!" shrieked Madame Rez. "There's a wild beast outside!" She scurried out of the door in a surprisingly unladylike manner.

Lulu giggled. She ran over to the window and opened it to look for Tufty. She spotted Clarabel, who was holding the wriggling cub in her arms.

"It's all right, she's gone now!" hissed Lulu. "You can come out."

Emily and Jaminta, who had been hiding around the corner, came over to join Clarabel.

"Sorry, Lulu!" said Jaminta. "Tufty slipped out of the bedroom when we opened the door."

"We had to chase him around the palace," added Clarabel. "Luckily no one saw us."

"Sorry to ruin your lesson!" Emily grinned.

Lulu rolled her eyes. "It was terrible! I felt about as ladylike as a giraffe! Now let's get out of here before someone spots Tufty."

Lulu slipped out of the door and beckoned them to follow her. Just as they were about to hurry away, they heard footsteps coming toward them.

"Where should we put Tufty?" whispered Clarabel.

Lulu looked around, but there was nothing in the hallway that would hide a wiggly lion cub. Then an idea struck her.

"Pass him to me," she said, taking Tufty from Clarabel's arms. Quick as a flash, she put him down on the floor and swung her skirts over him so that he was hidden underneath. Luckily, her long, frilly dress reached right down to the ground. She dropped her skirts just as Lady Malika swept around the corner.

"What are you all doing?" she asked, looking at the girls with narrowed eyes.

"Nothing," said Lulu.

"Really, nothing at all," added Emily.

Tufty gave a little meow beneath Lulu's dress, which Jaminta tried to drown out with a loud cough.

"It's nice to see you in a proper dress for a change, Lulu," said Lady Malika.

Lulu's skirts shook as Tufty bounced

around underneath, trying to find a way out. "Er . . . thank you, Aunt," she said.

Lady Malika frowned for a moment. Then she gave them one of her half smiles and walked away down the corridor.

"That was close!" whispered Emily.

Picking up Tufty, Lulu raced away, with the others following close behind.

💜

After taking the little lion cub back to Lulu's bedroom, the princesses hurried out in the truck with Ally to search the grasslands again. To their disappointment, there was still no sign of the lioness or the missing cubs.

As the sun began to set, they returned to the palace to eat dinner with the grown-ups and Prince Olaf. Afterward, they gathered in Lulu's room, wearing pajamas. Their jeweled rings glimmered on their fingers. It was a hot night, and the windows were flung wide open to try to catch any faint breeze.

"If only we'd found some kind of clue." Lulu sighed, folding up the map of the grasslands.

"Let's try again tomorrow," said Clarabel. "We'll find them somehow."

There was a knock at the door, and Ally entered carrying a tray of sugared marzipan shaped into little flowers and stars. The girls settled down on Lulu's bed to eat the candies. After his afternoon of mischief, Tufty had fallen fast asleep.

Ally crossed to the window to close the curtain, but stopped and gasped when the full moon came out from behind a cloud. As shafts of moonlight hit the mountain, its enormous black shape began to shine, until the whole peak transformed into glittering silver.

"What's wrong, Ally?" Lulu leaned

forward. In the moonlight she could see that Ally was very pale.

Ally stared at the mountain. "So that's why it's called Shimmer Rock! I'm sorry, Your Majesties," she smiled weakly. "It made me think of something from long ago."

"Why does Shimmer Rock sparkle like that, Lulu?" asked Jaminta.

"Well, the stories say that there's magic in the mountain," said Lulu. "But if you go right up to it and look closely, you can see millions of tiny crystals inside the stone. The moonlight makes the crystals shine."

"What is it, Ally? You look so strange!" Emily peered at her.

Ally hesitated. "I've heard about this mountain before," she said slowly. "Although I didn't know then that it was called Shimmer Rock. It all happened when I was working as an undercover agent searching for the missing Onica Heart Crystals."

"I remember you telling us about them before," said Emily. "You said they're the most famous missing jewels in the world!"

"They were the most prized treasure in my kingdom, a long time ago," added Jaminta, who came from Onica.

"That's right. They were very famous and highly prized jewels," agreed Ally. "I was told that they'd been crafted out of gems that came from a 'land of lions,' but it was a secret exactly where that was. Now I think that maybe it was here."

"Those Heart Crystals must be very beautiful," said Clarabel.

"Maybe jewels could help us find the missing lions." said Lulu excitedly. "How about your pearl, Clarabel? Remember

how you used it to find the dolphin last time? Maybe you could use it to find the lions."

Clarabel shook her head. "It's an ocean gem, so it only works for ocean creatures. Are there any other jewels that we could use, Jaminta?"

The princesses all looked hopefully at Jaminta. She had great skill at shaping gems to give them a special power, something she had learned from a master gem maker at home in the kingdom of Onica.

Jaminta pulled a velvet bag from her pocket, opened it, and poured a handful of glistening jewels onto the bed. "I can't think of anything that would help us. Here's the amethyst Clarabel chose from the treasure chest on Ampali Island. All I've done is polish it so far." She picked up the purple jewel and then yawned widely.

"But looking at it always seems to make me sleepy."

The other three girls looked at the sparkling purple jewel and yawned, too.

"How strange that a jewel would make us so sleepy!" Emily said, rubbing her eyes.

Ally took one last look at Shimmer Rock and closed the curtain. "Maybe you'll have some new ideas in the morning, Your Majesties. For now, I think you should get some sleep." She went to pick up the tray of marzipan but accidentally knocked it onto the floor with a clatter.

The noise woke Tufty, who jumped up in the air, landed on the floor, and scrambled under Lulu's frilly ball gown, which was lying in a heap. The dress rippled as he disappeared underneath it.

"Don't worry, Tufty. Everything's all right," said Lulu with a grin.

At the sound of her voice, Tufty stuck his whiskery nose out of an armhole, making the princesses burst out laughing.

Lulu scooped him up and kissed him. "Come on, little one. It's time for bed."

CHAPTER NINE

Night Ninjas

Lulu couldn't get to sleep that night. Through the open window came the buzz of insects and the distant yowl of a leopard. She kept thinking about the lion tracks and the empty hollow where the little cubs had lived. She shut her eyes tight, but sleep didn't come. It didn't help when Tufty jumped up on her bed and started nuzzling her cheek and purring deeply into her ear.

"Tufty!" she laughed, pushing him off.

"Are you trying to tell me you're hungry again?"

Tufty padded up and down the blanket, still purring. So, with a wide yawn, Lulu threw off the covers and climbed out of bed. She crept down the dark stairs and felt her way toward the kitchen. Everyone was in bed and all the rooms lay in quiet shadow.

Lulu filled the baby bottle up with milk from the refrigerator and fastened the lid back on. She smiled. This would stop Tufty from feeling hungry for a while. Turning to hurry back upstairs, she caught a glimpse of light through the window. It was round and yellow in the darkness.

Running to the window, Lulu looked out into the blackness.

A full moon turned the garden a shadowy silver. Beyond the high palace wall, Shimmer Rock glittered brightly.

Lulu stared at where the light had been. She saw it again, right over by the old gray wall next to the gardener's shed.

Suddenly, she realized that she'd seen a light in the same place from her bedroom window two nights ago. What could it be? Was it someone with a flashlight? Nobody should be out there in the garden. The palace guards always stayed by the gate, and everyone else was asleep.

She set the bottle of milk down on the kitchen table, her heart beating like an Undalan drum. Something strange was happening out there in the darkness. She dashed toward the stairs. It was time to wake the Rescue Princesses and find out exactly what was going on!

♥

The princesses slipped into light cotton dresses and plain silver tiaras, and crept silently down the corridor. A loud snoring came from Olaf's bedroom. Lulu looked at her friends and, trying hard not to giggle, they sneaked down the stairs and out into the dark courtyard.

"Where are we going?" whispered Emily.

"This way," hissed Lulu, leading them through an archway at the far end of the courtyard. Beyond the orange trees was the vegetable patch, and behind that was the high wall that surrounded the palace grounds.

"It really is such an amazing mountain!" said Clarabel, gazing at Shimmer Rock as it sparkled.

But Lulu had seen the mountain like that a thousand times, and hurried them on toward the shed. "The light came from right over here," she said.

Jaminta tried the shed door, but it was locked. "There's nothing here, Lulu. Are you sure you weren't dreaming?"

"Totally sure!" Lulu walked right up to the shed. "There used to be a huge pile of things here." She pointed at the ground on one side of the shed. "There were wheelbarrows, shovels, and sacks of dirt. But everything's been moved."

She stepped forward and her foot made a dull *thud* against the ground. She stopped, surprised.

"What was that?" said Clarabel nervously.

Lulu moved her other foot, which made a thudding noise, too.

"That's strange. It sounds really hollow," said Emily.

Kneeling down, Lulu swept her hand across the ground and found that the loose earth moved aside easily beneath her fingers. She continued brushing it away until she reached a solid rectangle of wood set into the ground.

"I didn't know there was anything under here," she cried. "It's always been covered up with gardening tools before."

"Not so loud," breathed Clarabel. "You'll wake the palace."

Jaminta knelt down beside her and tapped gently on the wooden rectangle. "It's like a door lying in the ground." She brushed more earth aside to reveal a ring-shaped handle made of metal and a small hole for a key. "Look! Here's the door handle and the lock."

"If it *is* a door, then let's open it," exclaimed Lulu.

"Shouldn't we figure out what it is first?" asked Clarabel.

Lulu was already yanking on the handle. The door gave a huge creak but held firmly shut.

"Let's all try pulling together!" said Emily.

So all the princesses grabbed the handle and heaved as hard as they could. But the door still wouldn't budge.

"We need the key," said Lulu. "But who would have it? No one knows this door is here."

"Someone must know," replied Jaminta. "I bet the person with the key is the same person you saw with a light."

Lulu looked around the garden. There was no sign of the light anymore. "I don't know who that could be. No one's ever talked about this."

She broke off suddenly. A strange noise came from below the wooden rectangle, making them jump.

"What was that?" said Emily.

Lulu crouched down and put her ear against the door. The other princesses did the same.

They waited for a moment, silent in
the darkness. Then the noise came again
from deep down, making the door shake.

The princesses jumped to their feet.

"There's an animal down there!"
Clarabel gasped.

"It's a lion," said Lulu, her eyes wide.
"That's the sound of a lion's roar."

CHAPTER TEN

The Door in the Ground

The princesses looked at one another excitedly.

"Maybe it's our missing lions!" cried Emily. "But why would they be underground?"

"We'll have to go down there and find out!" Lulu tugged on the handle again, but it wouldn't budge.

"I know something we can use to unlock it," said Jaminta. "Come on!"

The four girls raced back through

the moonlit courtyard into the palace. Jaminta stopped in the kitchen, searching through the silverware drawer. "It looks like an old lock. Maybe we can open it with a long piece of metal without needing the right key." She pulled out a fork with wide prongs. "This might do it."

The other princesses crowded around to look.

With a sudden *click*, the light went on, dazzling their eyes. They turned around in shock to find Prince Olaf standing in the kitchen doorway. He was wearing striped pajamas that were so big the sleeves hung over his hands.

"Hello," he said, beaming. "What's going on?"

"It's a . . . it's a . . ." stuttered Emily.

"It's a midnight feast," snapped Lulu.

"Yummy!" said Olaf, sitting down at the kitchen table. "Can I join you?"

Lulu watched him in horror. There, right in front of him, was the baby bottle with milk in it for Tufty. She'd left it there when she went out in the garden to search for the strange light.

Olaf picked it up. "What's this?"

The princesses exchanged glances.

"It's mine!" said Lulu defiantly. "I still like to drink milk like that." To prove it, she grabbed the baby bottle and took a huge slurp.

"Really? From a baby bottle?" said Olaf, looking puzzled.

"That's right," said Lulu, taking another drink. The bottle made a glugging sound. Emily gave a snort and turned away to hide her laughter.

With Olaf waiting expectantly for the midnight feast to begin, the girls began to look for some food. Clarabel found leftover pudding and spooned it into dishes. Lulu added some chocolate. They gulped theirs down, and then watched impatiently as Olaf ate his incredibly slowly.

Suddenly, footsteps sounded in the hallway. The princesses froze, listening as the steps came closer. They exchanged worried looks, but it was too late to clear everything away. The door swung open and Lady Malika walked into the room. "Princesses!" She raised her dark eyebrows in surprise. "What's going on, and why are you all dressed?"

"We're having a midnight feast," said the princesses, all at exactly the same time.

Lady Malika's eyebrows rose even higher. "Is everything all right, Lulu? I thought I heard a strange noise coming from your room, a sort of scratching sound. Is there something in there?"

"It was probably just a lizard walking on the roof," said Lulu quickly. "We should go upstairs and get some sleep now."

"Yes, I think you should," replied Lady Malika. "And you as well, Prince Olaf."

The girls trooped upstairs, said good night, and closed their doors. Lulu waited until she'd heard Olaf's bedroom door click shut and her aunt's door close, too. Then she opened hers a tiny crack. Emily, Clarabel, and Jaminta were peeking out of their rooms as well. Quietly, with their very best ninja steps, they prowled downstairs and out into the garden.

"I just hope this works on that lock," murmured Jaminta, tucking the fork she'd borrowed into her pocket.

The princesses reached the garden shed in seconds and crouched down next to the door in the ground. The rectangle of wood was easy to see now that its covering of earth was swept to one side. Jaminta wiggled one prong of the fork inside the lock. She twisted and jiggled, until finally there was a low *clunk*.

"I think I did it," she said. "Let's try the handle again."

Lulu and Emily grabbed the handle together and yanked it toward them. The rectangle of wood swung up with an enormous *creak*. A hole opened up in front of them, with broad stone steps stretching down into darkness.

"Where do you think it leads?" asked Clarabel.

"There's only one way to find out," replied Lulu, climbing down the steps. "But we have to be really quiet, in case a lion is loose down here."

Clarabel gulped, then she and Emily followed Lulu carefully down the steps.

Jaminta found a wheelbarrow and parked it in front of the hole.

"It won't hide the hole from close up," she explained to the others, "but at least it'll keep anyone from seeing it from far away. I don't want to pull the door shut in case we can't open it from the inside."

"Good idea," said Clarabel, shuddering at the thought of being trapped underground.

"We should have brought flashlights," Lulu called back.

"I brought my light bracelet. You take it, Lulu." Jaminta pulled an emerald bracelet from her pocket and passed it forward. The jewels lit up the tunnel with a bright green glow.

"Thanks!" Lulu held the bracelet in front of her and continued down the stone steps, followed by the others.

It seemed like a long way down. But when the stairs ended, they stood in a narrow tunnel with a floor of reddish earth. The air smelled musty.

They tiptoed through the passageway, finding their way by the light from the bracelet. At first the tunnel sloped down, until gradually it began to slope uphill again. The tunnel wall felt cool beneath Lulu's fingers.

"I wonder how far we've gone," murmured Emily.

"Hold on!" whispered Lulu. "I think I hear something."

They stopped and listened. A faint sound of meowing drifted down the tunnel.

"It sounds like Tufty when he wants some milk," said Clarabel.

Lulu's heart beat faster. "It must be the missing lion cubs!"

Running silently, the princesses followed the sound. The tunnel twisted and turned, and the meowing grew louder.

At last, Lulu stopped at a bend and held up her hand to signal the others to wait. Breathing fast, she peered around the corner. Half of her wanted to find the missing cubs quickly and hug them all tight. The other half of her knew that if the lioness was nearby, then they were all in danger. Terrible danger.

CHAPTER ELEVEN

The Hollow Mountain

At first, Lulu couldn't see anything except darkness. Determined to be brave, she lifted up the bracelet and cast emerald light around the corner. Ahead of her stretched a cavern so vast that she couldn't see across to the other side. The light from the jewels only just reached the high ceiling.

Something moved on one side of the cavern, and her heart missed a beat. "Oh no!" she cried. "The poor cubs!"

"What's wrong?" asked the others, crowding behind her.

A small metal cage stood on the earthen floor, with the lioness and four cubs trapped inside it. The cubs moved restlessly, tumbling over one another and meowing. The lioness lay still, her eyes staring into the darkness.

Lulu ran toward the cage. But as she got close the lioness stiffened, then sprang up and snarled. Lulu stopped and backed away a little.

"She doesn't know we're trying to help her," said Clarabel.

Lulu's eyes flashed. "Whoever did this doesn't care about animals at all! How could they put wild lions into a tiny cage like that?"

"The poor cubs look so unhappy," said Clarabel, her blue eyes sad.

Lulu walked carefully around the cage until she found the side with the door.

"Stop, Lulu!" cried Emily. "The lioness could hurt us if we let them out. We need to find another way to do this!"

Lulu put her hands on her hips. She knew Emily was right. Walter had talked to her about safety many times.

"Look at this!" said Jaminta suddenly, touching the wall and gazing at her hand. Her fingers were covered with sparkling crystals.

"I know where we are!" Lulu gasped. "We're inside Shimmer Rock. The stories about the mountain being hollow must be true."

The princesses gazed around them. Instead of reddish earth, the walls of the cavern were studded with millions of little crystals, just like the ones that shimmered when moonlight struck the mountain.

"There are more cages over here."
Jaminta took the emerald bracelet from
Lulu and shone it all around the cavern,
revealing more metal cages, all standing
empty. "Here's another tunnel. I bet it
leads out to the grasslands. That's how
someone brought the animals in here."

Lulu looked at the metal bars of the
lions' cage. "We need to find a way to
let the lions out that still gives us time
to get away."

"I know something that might work,"
said Emily, shaking back her red hair.
"Remember how looking at the purple
amethyst gem made us feel sleepy? We
could see if it has the same effect on the
lions."

"Do you really think that will work?"
asked Clarabel.

"Maybe," said Jaminta thoughtfully.
"If they fall asleep, we can open the door

safely. When they wake up again they can leave the cage by themselves."

"That's a great idea!" cried Lulu, making the lioness growl again. "Then they'll find their way to the tunnel that leads to the grasslands. Lions have a really good sense of smell."

"Lulu and I can go get the jewel," said Jaminta.

"We'll hide here and keep watch in case the lion stealers come back," said Emily, and Clarabel nodded in agreement.

Lulu and Jaminta ran from the cavern, their feet thudding through the black tunnel. They'd left the emerald bracelet with Emily and Clarabel, so they kept a hand on the wall of the passageway to steady themselves. Dashing up the steps, they climbed out of the hole and ran across the garden. The full moon hung above the palace, and the call of a leopard drifted over from the grasslands.

Upstairs, they began searching for the amethyst in Jaminta's bedroom.

"I'm sure I put it in here," whispered Jaminta, opening a drawer and pulling out a small velvet bag.

Lulu held out her hand and Jaminta dropped the amethyst into it. Turning it over in her fingers, Lulu noticed its hexagonal shape and its heart of deepest purple. She yawned widely, covering her mouth with her hand.

"The jewel works really fast," she muttered to Jaminta, quickly putting it back in the velvet bag before she became any sleepier.

They were rushing out of Jaminta's room toward the stairs, when Lulu noticed her own bedroom door standing wide open.

Her stomach turned over. The door should be shut. She knew she'd closed it, so that Tufty didn't get loose.

"Oh no, where's Tufty?" she hissed, running inside. "Tufty! Where are you?" Her eyes flicked anxiously around the room.

"Maybe he's hiding," said Jaminta, looking behind a dresser.

Lulu pulled back her bed sheets, looking in her bed and then underneath it. Then she searched her closet, her drawers, and everywhere else she could think of.

Tufty was nowhere.

"I can't believe it. He disappeared." With tears pricking the back of her eyes, Lulu sank down onto her bed. Tufty could be lost in the palace, or someone could have taken him away. Where should she go to keep looking for him?

The *creak* of a floorboard made her

turn around. Olaf was standing in the doorway.

Lulu leapt up. "Did you come in here tonight? Did you leave my door open?" she said fiercely.

Olaf's spiky hair looked silvery in the moonlight. "It wasn't me, but I did see somebody come in here. I watched them through a crack in my door. But it was too dark to see who it was." He pushed up his baggy pajama sleeves.

"Did you hear anything strange?" asked Jaminta.

"There was a noise that sounded like an animal," said Olaf.

"Tufty!" said Lulu sadly. "He's a lion cub who lost his family."

Olaf chuckled. "Were you taking care of him? I thought that you princesses were up to something! I guess that's what the baby bottle was for, then?"

Lulu nodded, a hollow feeling growing inside her. She missed Tufty already.

"You can't give up on him now," said Olaf. "Here, take my flashlight and this chocolate. When the kings and queens wake up, I'll tell them that you and your friends went for an early drive across the grasslands with Ally. That'll give you lots of time to find him."

Lulu stared at him. "You'd cover for us? After the way I've been really grumpy with you?"

"It would be my pleasure!" said Olaf, bowing grandly.

Lulu bit her lip to stop a smile. He looked so funny bowing in those baggy pajamas. But underneath, she felt awful about how she'd treated him. He'd seemed annoying, but now she could see he was actually very kind.

"Thank you, Olaf," said Jaminta, taking the flashlight.

Lulu put the chocolate bar in her pocket and patted Olaf on the shoulder. "I'm really sorry I've been so snappy with you. When all this is over, you can use my gymnastics equipment as much as you want!"

Olaf smiled and bowed again. "Good luck, princesses!"

CHAPTER TWELVE

The Sleep Jewel

Lulu and Jaminta crept back out into the courtyard, pausing by the fountain.

"The person who stole Tufty must be the same person who captured the other lions," cried Lulu. "They could be driving away with him right now!"

"I know," said Jaminta. "But I think we should take the amethyst gem to Emily and Clarabel, and tell them what's going on."

They climbed down into the hole and

turned on Olaf's flashlight. Going down the steps and along the passageway would be much easier now that they had a light. They sprinted down the tunnel, the light bouncing as they ran. Turning the corner, they stopped inside the vast cavern with its walls of glittering crystals. Emily and Clarabel hurried over to meet them.

"Did you find the amethyst?" asked Clarabel.

Lulu held it out to show them, as she tried to catch her breath. "Don't look at it for too long," she warned them. "It makes you sleepy really fast."

"We explored the cavern and found another way out," Emily told her. "There's a wider tunnel that leads to the foot of the mountain."

"We're sure that the lioness will catch the scent of the grasslands and escape that way," added Clarabel.

"Great! After we've released these lions, we have to go and look for Tufty," said Lulu, and she explained how Olaf had seen someone take the little cub from her room.

"Poor Tufty! There's no time to lose!" said Emily. "Let's see if the amethyst works."

Lulu crept toward the lions' cage with the amethyst hidden in the palm of her hand. The little cubs took no notice of her. But as she came closer, the lioness began a long, low growl. Crouching down slowly, Lulu laid the amethyst next to the bars of the cage. The lioness stared at it and the cubs bounced over to look, spellbound by its sparkling purple shape.

Lulu hurried back to the others and made them turn away from the jewel.

"If we're not careful, we'll end up staring at it," she hissed. "Then we'll fall asleep, too." She nudged Clarabel, who was taking a sideways peek at the amethyst.

The minutes seemed endless as they waited. Finally, when the cave felt very still and quiet, Lulu dared to peek around.

"It worked!" she whispered.

All the lions were still, their furry golden bodies stretched out peacefully. Even the lioness had laid her head on the ground, her eyes shut tight.

Clarabel smiled. "The cubs look even cuter when they're sleeping."

"We have to be quick," said Jaminta. "We don't know how long they'll sleep for."

Lulu strode up to the cage door. But just as she was about to open it, footsteps came from the other end of the cave. She turned Olaf's flashlight toward the sound, and a figure emerged from a tunnel, carrying a bundle.

Lulu's mouth dropped open. It was Lady Malika.

When she saw the girls, Lady Malika stopped, her face twisting furiously.

"I don't believe it!" whispered Emily.

But Lulu couldn't speak. How could the thief be her aunt? It didn't make sense. Then she remembered how her aunt had wanted the princesses to come and visit her, so that they would stay away from the grasslands. Her aunt had been awake last night, too, and could easily have taken Tufty.

"What are you nosy girls doing here?" snapped Lady Malika, her voice echoing around the cavern. "These are my beasts! I captured them and brought them here in my truck, ready to be put to work in the circus. I won't have you meddlesome princesses getting in my way!"

Lulu recovered her voice. "You're not taking them anywhere, and we'll tell the king and queen unless you leave right now!"

"Dreadful princesses!" screeched Lady Malika. Then she dropped her bundle on the floor, turned on her heels, and fled back into the shadows.

Lulu breathed in sharply. Was the bundle what she hoped it would be? She raced across the cavern. Scooping it up, she kissed the furry ears and wriggly body of a little lion cub.

"Tufty! It's really you!" She beamed at him in delight.

Inside the cage, the lioness rolled over with a grunt but didn't open her eyes.

"Quickly, Lulu!" whispered Jaminta.

Holding Tufty under one arm, Lulu undid the latch of the cage and pulled. But the door didn't budge.

"There's a second latch, really high up," said Emily, pointing at it.

Lulu put Tufty into Clarabel's arms and stretched up to reach the other door latch. "I — can't — get — to — it!" she said between clenched teeth.

Looking around, she noticed a piece of rock jutting out of the wall near the cage. She scrambled up onto it and looked down on the metal bars below her.

"Wait, Lulu! You aren't going to jump, are you?" called Clarabel.

"I have to," replied Lulu. Keeping her eyes on the metal roof, she made an enormous leap off the rock to land on the top of the cage with a *bang*. The lioness below her opened her eyes, then shut them again.

Holding her breath, Lulu crawled to

the edge of the bars, stretched over, and flicked open the latch. Then she stood up, backflipped off the roof, and landed gracefully on the ground.

Jaminta swung the cage door open. Clarabel handed Tufty back to Lulu, who kissed him one more time and placed him gently in the cage. He scampered up to his brothers and sisters and lay down next to them with a happy meow. Lulu left the cage door open and backed away.

"Ready?" asked Jaminta, preparing to grab the amethyst.

Lulu looked at Tufty. She didn't want to leave him, but she knew she had to give him this chance to be a wild cub again. "Yes, ready!" she said.

Jaminta grabbed the purple gem and they tiptoed out of the cavern. They crept around the corner into the narrow tunnel and broke into a run. Clarabel stumbled over a loose rock, but Lulu helped her up. Sprinting hard, they didn't stop until they reached the bottom of the stone steps that led to the palace garden. A square of yellow light at the top told them that the sun would soon be rising.

The princesses paused, trying to catch their breath.

A deafening roar swept down the tunnel, making the floor and walls tremble.

"The lioness!" cried Lulu. "She woke up."

They climbed as fast as they could and scrambled out of the hole at the top. Then together they heaved the old wooden door shut and pushed a wheelbarrow right on top of it, just to be sure that nothing could get out that way.

"We did it!" Emily bounced up and down. "We freed all the lions!"

"And Tufty got his family back again," said Lulu.

As Jaminta tucked the amethyst sleep jewel away in her pocket, Clarabel noticed something else in her hand. "What's that you're holding, Jaminta?" she asked.

Jaminta held out one hand to show them dozens of sparkling stones. "I picked up some crystals inside the cave. I'm going to try making powerful jewels with them. If the Onica Heart Crystals were made from stones like these, they must be really special."

A golden sun peeked over the horizon, sending a warm glow across the palace garden. The princesses sat down on the ground, their legs aching.

Lulu fumbled in her pocket and pulled out the chocolate that Olaf had given her. She broke off big pieces and handed them around. The chocolate tasted especially sweet after all that running down the tunnel.

"What a strange mystery that was," said Emily. "The lions were hidden under the mountain all this time."

"Not anymore." Lulu smiled, her eyes sparkling. "I bet they're already heading back to the grasslands, where they belong."

CHAPTER THIRTEEN

A Royal Circus Show

The princesses stumbled, yawning, into breakfast that morning. They'd changed out of their dusty clothes into long silk dresses and their favorite tiaras, hoping that the kings and queens wouldn't notice anything different.

Lulu shook back her curly black hair as she sat down at the table. She felt so sleepy, but a large helping of pancakes and syrup began to make her feel better.

"I hope the etiquette lessons aren't tiring you out, Lulu," said Queen Shani, looking at the dark circles under her daughter's eyes.

Lulu glanced at the other princesses and bit her lip to hide a smile. "Not really. But maybe I should take a break from them for a little while."

"Just for a little while." The queen nodded and turned to her husband. "I'm just so disappointed with Lady Malika."

"Yes, dear," replied the king, passing her the teapot. "I'm glad she was caught."

"Huh? What's that?" Lulu's lionlike eyes flashed at the mention of her aunt.

"Please speak gently, my dear," said the queen. "We received a message from Walter this morning. He found several wild animals from the grasslands in Lady Malika's circus, mainly zebras and leopards. She must have taken them from here by truck. Thankfully, those animals are back in the wild now and the circus has been closed."

The princesses exchanged looks. Lady Malika had wanted the lions to perform in her circus, too. At least now she couldn't hurt any more animals.

"I think circuses should just have human performers," said Olaf loudly. "I'd love to show you the circus skills I've been practicing."

Lulu beamed at him. For a prince, Olaf was pretty decent. "Why don't we do circus skills together? All five of us," she said. "We'll practice this morning and put on a show after lunch."

"I'll juggle!" cried Emily.

"I'll walk on stilts," added Jaminta.

Clarabel frowned for a moment, then smiled mysteriously.

After lunch, the table was moved from the Great Hall and the kings and queens of Undala and Finia, and Lulu's etiquette teacher, Madame Rez, sat down to watch the circus show.

First, Olaf walked along the balance beam. Then Lulu followed him with a series of tumbles across the floor, ending with a backflip. Emily and Jaminta put on good displays of juggling and stilt-walking. Then a funny figure with a red nose and enormous checkered trousers wobbled in, and started falling over and making the audience burst out laughing.

Lulu grinned to see Clarabel performing so well as a clown. When the clown act had ended, Lulu finished off the show by walking on her hands in front of the audience while balancing a book on her feet.

"Bravo!" cried Madame Rez. "Magnificent show, Lulu! You can balance the book on your feet in our next lesson."

When all the clapping had died down, Queen Shani rose from her seat. "Well done, all of you! Lulu, we're very proud of your acrobatic skills, and this seems like the perfect time to give this to you." She handed a wrapped package to her daughter.

Surprised, Lulu tore open the paper and pulled out a beautiful yellow leotard decorated with golden star sequins. The princesses gathered around to admire it.

"Now you can practice your acrobatics while looking like a real gymnast," explained the king.

"It's fantastic! Thank you," said Lulu, giving her parents a hug.

The princesses and Olaf watched the sun set on the grasslands that evening. Ally drove them up to the hollow to see the lioness and her cubs in their grassland home once more. A herd of elephants wandered past, kicking up the reddish earth, and, in the distance, giraffes were eating from the trees. The princesses watched the lion cubs happily.

"I'm so glad they found their way back," said Clarabel.

"They look so happy," added Emily.

Lulu smiled as Tufty chased his brothers and sisters around and around. He stopped and gazed at her for a moment with his big brown eyes. Then he scampered through the bushes.

"Where's the lioness? I wish I could see her as well," said Olaf.

"She's probably lying down," said Lulu.

"If you climb up the tree, you'll get a good view from there."

The princesses had to help him up a little. But after some shoving, Olaf managed to climb up the tree. "You're right! I've got a great view from up here." His voice was faint as he called down from the very top.

Lulu grinned at her friends. "For a prince, he's really not that bad."

"He's definitely one of the good ones," agreed Jaminta, taking the Shimmer Rock crystals from her pocket for another look.

"Be careful with those stones," said Ally from the driver's seat. "If you join them together they'll be very valuable and powerful, just like the Onica Heart Crystals."

"Don't worry. We'll be careful," said Jaminta.

"But we like to be adventurous, too," said Lulu, swinging herself into the tree and hanging upside down.

"I don't know which is wilder, Lulu. You or the lion cubs." Ally laughed.

"There's nothing wilder than a Rescue Princess!" said Lulu.